Rapunzel and the Golden Rule

By Barbara Bazaldua

Illustrated by STUDIO IBOIX

Random House New York

Copyright © 2011 Disney Enterprises, Inc. All rights reserved. Published in the United States by Random House Children's Books, a division of Random House, Inc., 1745 Broadway, New York, NY 10019, and in Canada by Random House of Canada Limited, Toronto, in conjunction with Disney Enterprises, Inc. Random House and the colophon are registered trademarks of Random House, Inc.

ISBN: 978-0-7364-2829-3

www.randomhouse.com/kids

MANUFACTURED IN CHINA

10 9 8 7 6 5 4 3 2

*R*apunzel was about to see her lifelong dream come true! She had just ventured out of her tall tower for the very first time. A young man named Flynn was taking her to the kingdom to see the floating lights that appeared in the sky every year on her birthday. Unfortunately, a horse named Maximus appeared—and tried to drag Flynn away!

Flynn had stolen something from the palace, and the palace horse Maximus was determined to arrest him. Luckily, Rapunzel persuaded Maximus to let Flynn go—at least until after she had seen the floating lights. But when Flynn tried to climb onto Maximus's back, the horse threw him into the mud!

"I don't like this horse," Flynn said.
"And this horse doesn't like me."

Rapunzel was sure she could teach Flynn and Maximus to like each other. But she knew it wasn't going to be easy. . . .

Rapunzel explained the golden rule to Flynn and Maximus. To get along, they needed to treat each other in the same way that they themselves would like to be treated. That meant they had to be nice to each other! To demonstrate, Rapunzel scratched Maximus's ears.

"See?" she asked Flynn. "Now you do it."

Flynn reluctantly patted Maximus on the head. Rapunzel
was thrilled that they were getting along better already.
"Now let's all go to the kingdom together," she said.

Entering the kingdom was a little tricky, since Flynn was wanted by the palace guards. But Maximus let the young man hide behind him as they walked past the guards. Flynn was very grateful for the horse's help.

That day, Maximus kept a sharp
eye on Flynn so that he wouldn't try
to escape. The horse was surprised
when he saw the young man being
kind to Rapunzel and the animals
of the kingdom. And soon Maximus
began to realize that maybe Flynn
wasn't so bad after all. . . .

Later that evening, something terrible happened. Rapunzel was taken away and locked up in her hidden tower! Flynn and Maximus knew they had to work together to rescue her.

Working as a team, Maximus and Flynn found the hidden tower—and saved their friend Rapunzel!

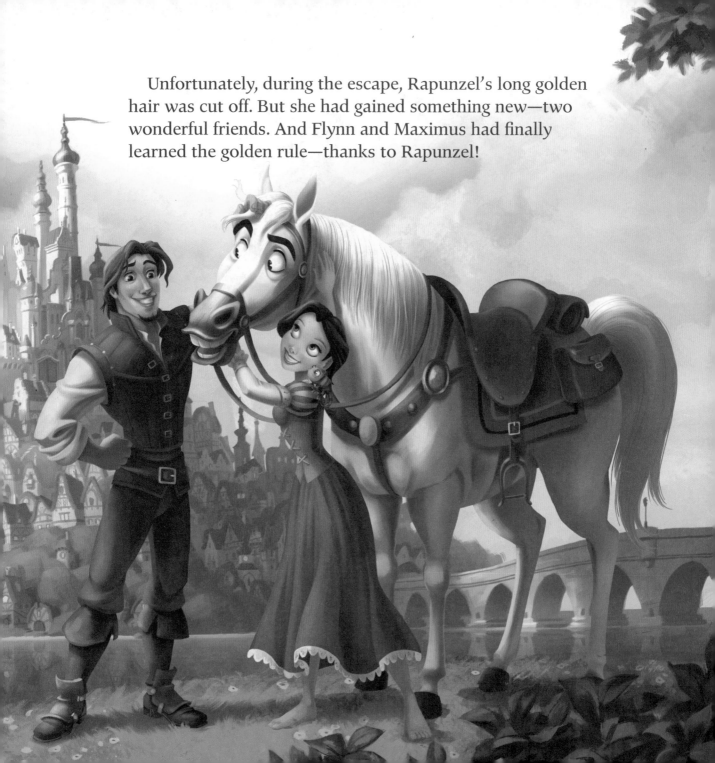

Unfortunately, during the escape, Rapunzel's long golden hair was cut off. But she had gained something new—two wonderful friends. And Flynn and Maximus had finally learned the golden rule—thanks to Rapunzel!

The very next morning, the circus tent was moved right next to Jasmine's palace! Mallika could perform at the royal circus every day and come home to Rajah every evening.

A royal ball was held to celebrate. And everyone—Jasmine and Aladdin, the circus owner, and the two tigers—lived happily ever after.

The two tigers ran to each other and gently touched noses.

Jasmine and Aladdin were very happy for Rajah and Mallika. But they felt bad for the circus owner. Without his star tigress, the circus would surely close.

Suddenly, Jasmine had a wonderful idea. . . .

That night, there was a knock at the palace door. It was the circus owner—and a very sad-looking tigress.

"Ever since Rajah left the circus, Mallika won't eat," the circus owner said. "Even though she's the star of my show, I want her to be happy. So I've come to give her to you."

The next day at the palace, Rajah was miserable.
Jasmine had the royal animal keeper bring in a line of tigers
to keep Rajah company.
But none of them could take
the place of Mallika.

When the show was over, Jasmine and Aladdin took Rajah to meet Mallika. The two tigers were very happy to be together—and clearly did not want to be apart.

"Can Mallika please come live at my palace?" Jasmine asked the circus owner. "She would be very happy there."

"I'm sorry, Mallika is our star," the owner replied. "Without her, there wouldn't be a circus."

Inside the circus tent, the announcer said, "I now present Mallika—
the star of our show!" And out walked a beautiful tigress.
Jasmine saw Rajah's face light up. He was in love!

Soon Jasmine, Aladdin, Apu, and Rajah were riding through Agrabah in the royal carriage. As they rolled past the circus poster, the tiger suddenly perked up.

"Hmmm," Aladdin said. "Maybe we should take Rajah to the circus."

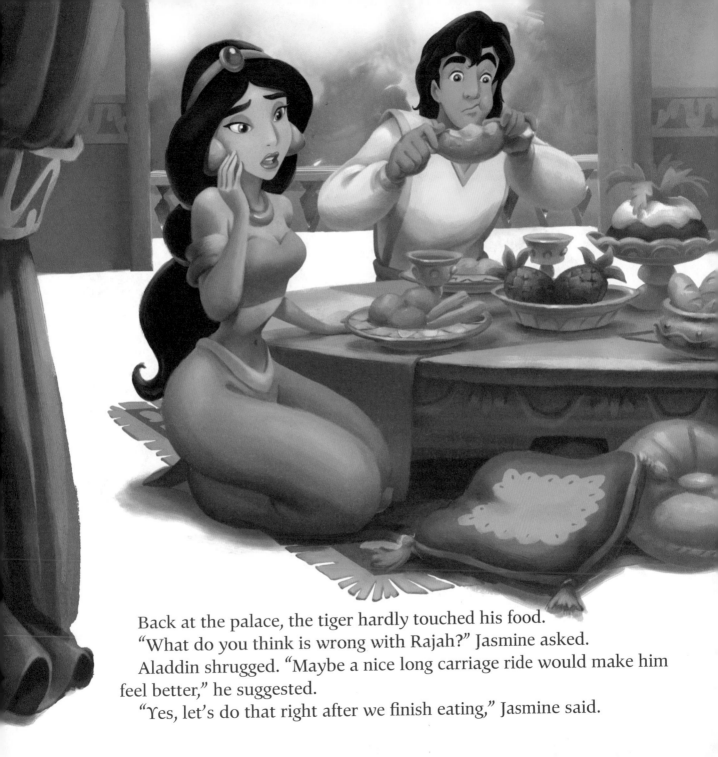

Back at the palace, the tiger hardly touched his food.

"What do you think is wrong with Rajah?" Jasmine asked.

Aladdin shrugged. "Maybe a nice long carriage ride would make him feel better," he suggested.

"Yes, let's do that right after we finish eating," Jasmine said.

One morning, Princess Jasmine and her pet tiger, Rajah, were riding through the busy streets of Agrabah. They came upon a big, colorful circus tent that had been put up the night before. The tiger's eyes opened wide as he stared at the circus poster.

"That looks like fun," Jasmine said to Rajah. "But we really should be going. It's almost time for lunch."

Jasmine and the Two Tigers

By Lara Bergen

Illustrated by STUDIO IBOIX

Random House New York

ISBN: 978-0-7364-2829-3
www.randomhouse.com/kids
MANUFACTURED IN CHINA
10 9 8 7 6 5 4 3 2